MW00997139

PEAS

by Nicholas Heller

Greenwillow Books, New York

For Kiira

Watercolor paints and a black pen line were used for
the full-color art. The text type is Neuzeit S Book.

Copyright © 1993 by Nicholas Heller. All rights reserved.
No part of this book may be reproduced or utilized in any
form or by any means, electronic or mechanical, including
photocopying, recording, or by any information storage and
retrieval system, without permission in writing from the
Publisher, Greenwillow Books, a division of William Morrow
& Company, Inc., 1350 Avenue of the Americas,
New York, NY 10019.

Printed in Singapore by Tien Wah Press
First Edition   10 9 8 7 6 5 4 3 2 1

Library of Congress Cataloging-in-Publication Data
Heller, Nicholas.
Peas / by Nicholas Heller.
            p.   cm.
Summary: After refusing to eat his peas, Lewis dreams that they
get out of their bowl and go for a wild ride on his electric train.
ISBN 0-688-12406-2 (trade). ISBN 0-688-12407-0 (lib. bdg.)
[1. Peas–Fiction.   2. Food habits–Fiction.   3. Railroads–Fiction.
4. Toys–Fiction.   5. Dreams–Fiction.]   I. Title.   PZ7.H37426Pe   1993
      [E]–dc20   92-29740   CIP   AC

CHAPTER ONE

Lewis didn't like peas.
"Yuck!" he said, and pushed them away.

"But peas taste good," said his mother, "and
they are good for you. Besides," she added,
"you'll hurt their feelings if you don't eat
them!"

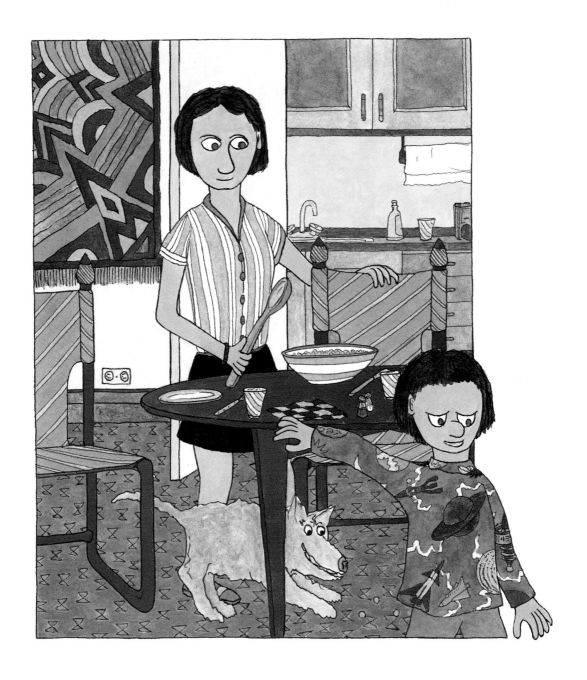

"Peas don't have feelings," Lewis said. "May I be excused now?"

"All right," said his mother. "I'll just save the peas for tomorrow."

"I won't eat them tomorrow, either," Lewis called from somewhere in the other room.

Lewis did some homework

and played with the dog.

He made a few adjustments to
his electric train set,

and then he went to bed and fell asleep.

CHAPTER TWO

The peas were downstairs in a bowl on the kitchen counter.

By and by, as the house grew quiet, one of the peas yawned and stretched and announced, "I'm bored. We've been sitting here for hours, and no one has eaten us yet."

"Well, then, come on!" said a big fat pea.
"Let's go find something else to do. Follow
  me!"
  The peas slipped over the rim of their bowl,
  leaped off the counter, and scampered
  across the kitchen floor.

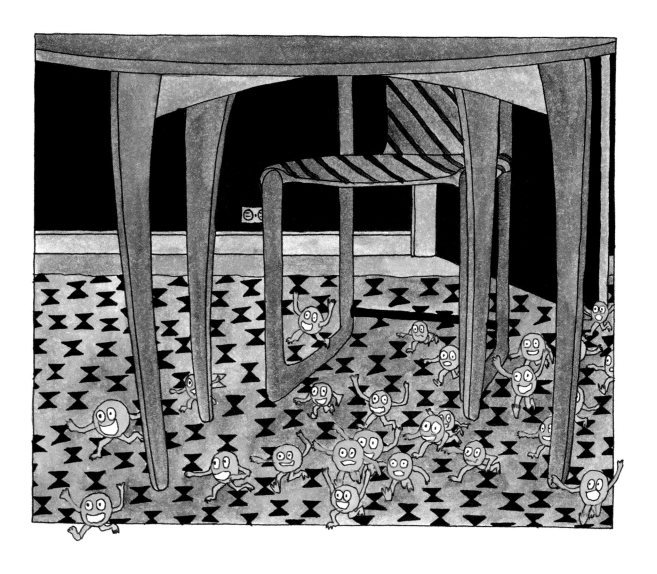

"Whee! Yippee!" squealed the peas as they
scurried under the dinner table.

"Come on!" shouted the fat pea as they tumbled around the corner into the living room.

"Wow! A train!" squeaked the peas. "Let's go for a ride. We'll go somewhere where we're appreciated!"

"I get to be engineer!" shouted the fat pea.
"And I'm the conductor!" said another.
"I'll be the signalman!" screamed a third.

"No! *I* want to be the signalman!" shouted another pea, and it knocked over the signal post.

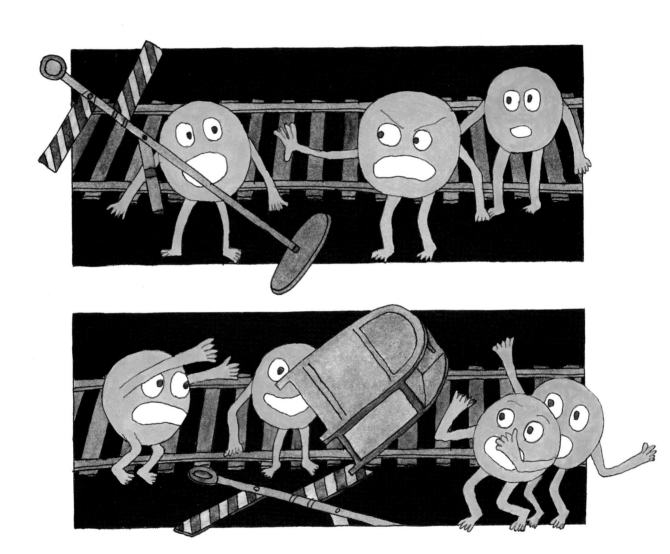

"Hey, cut it out over there!" yelled an angry pea, and it threw a toy mailbox at them.

"Off we go! Hurrah!" called the engineer as the train pulled out of the station. "Wait!" cried the conductor. "The passengers aren't aboard yet!" But the engineer paid no attention.

"This will stop him!" yelled a bunch of peas
as they pushed a toy truck onto the tracks.

Crash! The train hit the truck and sent it
bouncing into the station!

Clunkety-clunk! The train derailed. It slid
into a wooden cow — Bang! — and then
knocked over some plastic trees.
"Look what you've done!" squealed a little
pea. "We're stuck here now! We'll never get
to be eaten!"

CHAPTER THREE

Lewis woke up with a start. It was morning.
"I had the strangest dream," he told the dog
as they ran into the living room.

"At least, I think it was a dream. But I just
want to make sure," Lewis said as he
inspected his electric train set.
"Make sure about what?" called his mother
from the kitchen.

"About the peas," said Lewis. "Do you really
think I hurt their feelings by not eating them?"

"Peas don't have feelings, silly!" said Lewis's
  mother.
"Just the same," said Lewis, "I think I'd like
  peas for breakfast, please."

"Yuck!" said Lewis after his first bite. "I'm glad they don't have feelings, because I really don't like peas!"
But he ate them all up, anyway.